ALIENS and UFOs

Theo Baker

Rourke Educational Media

rourkeeducationalmedia.com

Before, During, and After Reading Activities

Before Reading: Building Background Knowledge and Academic Vocabulary

"Before Reading" strategies activate prior knowledge and set a purpose for reading. Before reading a book, it is important to tap into what your child or students already know about the topic. This will help them develop their vocabulary and increase their reading comprehension.

Questions and activities to build background knowledge:

1. *Look at the cover of the book. What will this book be about?*
2. *What do you already know about the topic?*
3. *Let's study the Table of Contents. What will you learn about in the book's chapters?*
4. *What would you like to learn about this topic? Do you think you might learn about it from this book? Why or why not?*

Building Academic Vocabulary

Building academic vocabulary is critical to understanding subject content.
Assist your child or students to gain meaning of the following vocabulary words.

Content Area Vocabulary

Read the list. What do these words mean?

- *craft*
- *extraordinary*
- *groggy*
- *hovered*
- *teeming*
- *witnesses*

During Reading: Writing Component

"During Reading" strategies help to make connections, monitor understanding, generate questions, and stay focused.

1. *While reading, write in your reading journal any questions you have or anything you do not understand.*
2. *After completing each chapter, write a summary of the chapter in your reading journal.*
3. *While reading, make connections with the text and write them in your reading journal.*
   a) Text to Self – What does this remind me of in my life? What were my feelings when I read this?
   b) Text to Text – What does this remind me of in another book I've read? How is this different from other books I've read?
   c) Text to World – What does this remind me of in the real world? Have I heard about this before? (News, current events, school, etc....)

After Reading: Comprehension and Extension Activity

"After Reading" strategies provide an opportunity to summarize, question, reflect, discuss, and respond to text. After reading the book, work on the following questions with your child or students to check their level of reading comprehension and content mastery.

1. Who are the "Men in Black"? *(Summarize)*
2. Why did the rancher in Roswell think the crash debris was interesting? *(Infer)*
3. Why is it a great challenge to travel to other stars? *(Asking Questions)*
4. What would you do if you saw a UFO? *(Text to Self Connection)*

Extension Activity

Want to dig deeper into the UFO mystery? Ask people you know. Poll your friends and family members. Ask whether they've ever seen a UFO. If anyone has, take their report and investigate it. Ask questions. Make sketches. Return to the scene with an adult's supervision. Try to identify the unidentified.

Table of Contents

Early Visitors

The universe is vast and ancient. It could be **teeming** with intelligent life. And it's possible that aliens from across the galaxy have visited Earth.

teeming (TEE-ming): to be filled or overflowing

The SETI Institute

The SETI Institute in California researches the possibility of extraterrestrial life. Extraterrestrial means “life beyond Earth.”

The Dogon tribe in Mali claim that thousands of years ago, they were visited by beings from the star Sirius. These beings, called Nommos, told them that Sirius had a twin star, invisible to the naked eye. In 1970, this twin star, Sirius B, was photographed by scientists.

Sirius is the brightest star visible from Earth.

Members of the Dogon tribe perform the ancient dama dance. They say this dance is a bridge to another world.

In the late 1800s, thousands of people began to see strange ships in the sky. These long, glowing ships flew silently through the night. Some people claimed they saw odd, non-human figures flying these **craft**.

craft (kraft): ships, aircraft, or other vessels

The Stars Are Far

Our spaceships have left Earth and traveled to the moon. The trip takes about three days. But if we wanted to blast to Proxima Centauri, the nearest star, using our fastest rockets, the trip would take nearly 6,300 years!

Kansas farmer Alexander Hamilton spotted a long ship flying over his fields. The craft **hovered** above one of the farmer's favorite cows. The ship dropped down a cable, which wrapped around the cow's neck. As Alexander watched, the ship rose back into the sky with his prized cow.

hovered (HUHV-urd): stayed in one place in the air

The Atomic Age

Kenneth Arnold was flying his private plane when he saw nine shining disks weaving in and out of the clouds. The local newspaper called these objects "flying saucers."

PAGE 2 THE CHICAGO SUN, THURSDAY, JUNE 26, 1947

In These United States

Supersonic Flying Saucers Sighted by Idaho Pilot

Speed Estimated at 1,200 Miles an Hour When Seen 10,000 Feet Up Near Mt. Rainier

In 1947, a rancher discovered strange crash debris in his fields in Roswell, New Mexico. He thought it might have been a flying saucer. The U.S. Army said it was a crashed weather balloon.

Roswell Daily Record

RECORD PHONES
Business Office 2288
News Department 2287

ROSWELL, NEW MEXICO, TUESDAY, JULY 8, 1947

RAAF Captures Flying Saucer On Ranch in Roswell Region

Claims Army Is Stacking Courts Martial

Indiana Senator Lays Protest Before Patterson

House Passes Tax Slash by Large Margin

Defeat Amendment By Demos to Remove Many from Rolls

Security Council Paves Way to Talks On Arms Reductions

No Details of Flying Disk Are Revealed

Roswell Hardware Man and Wife Report Disk Seen

Ex-King Carol Weds Mme. Lupescu

Former King Carol of Romania and Mme. Elena Lupescu relax aboard the S. S. America bound for Cuba and Mexico in May, 1941. A member of Carol's household in Rio de Janeiro said the ex-king and his companion for 23 years in reign and exile were recently married at their hotel Copacabana Palace suite. (AP Wirephoto).

Miners and Operators Sign Highest Wage Pact in History

American League Wins All-Star Game

...of Soviet Satellites May Attend Paris Meeting

In 1948, an experienced fighter pilot chased after a large, glowing craft. The craft swirled and dove. It seemed to reach impossible speeds as it rose into the sky. The pilot blacked out, and his plane crashed on a Kentucky farm.

The U.S. government investigated thousands of flying saucer sighting reports. Officials said there was nothing unusual about most of the saucer sightings. But some remained unexplained. They called them Unidentified Flying Objects, or UFOs.

Many reports of UFOs were from trained observers: police officers, pilots, and radar technicians.

Project Blue Book

Project Blue Book was a U.S. Air Force investigation to determine if UFOs were a national security threat. After nearly 20 years of study, the project found no evidence that UFOs were a threat, nor that they belonged to alien beings.

People have long suspected the U.S. government hides alien bodies and spacecraft at a place called Area 51 in Nevada. In 2013, the CIA said Area 51 was a secret site used to test aerial surveillance technology, not to hide aliens.

NELLIS BOMBING AND GUNNERY RANGE
RESTRICTED AREA
NO TRESPASSING
BEYOND THIS POINT
PHOTOGRAPHY IS PROHIBITED
WARNING
Restricted Area

I Met an Alien

Witnesses to UFO landings often claimed they saw aliens standing still within glowing lights. Some reports include sightings of aliens carrying "toolboxes," digging in the ground, hovering, and even repairing their ships.

Hit and Run

David Morris saw a large, cone-shaped object hovering over a wheat field. He slowed to watch it. Then he saw five small, gray beings dressed in orange jumpsuits running across the road. Overcome with terror, Morris fled the scene.

witnesses (WIT-nis-es): people who have personal knowledge of something

In 1961, a married couple followed a UFO while they drove home. The couple heard a strange beeping sound, became **groggy**, and blacked out. When they came to, they were still driving, but it was two hours later.

groggy (GROG-ee): dazed and weakened, as if tired

The couple claimed aliens took them aboard the UFO and ran medical tests on them.

After reporting a UFO, some people say they were visited by men wearing all black claiming to be government investigators. But many said these men were not normal. Some had strange eyes, others had trouble breathing. All seemed inhuman.

A Hoax?

The public first learned of the "Men in Black" in Gray Barker's 1956 book, *They Knew Too Much About Flying Saucers*.

Even with new camera technology, no one has managed to take a detailed photo of a UFO or an alien. That doesn't mean they don't exist, but it's good to remember the words of scientist Dr. Carl Sagan: "**Extraordinary** claims call for extraordinary evidence."

extraordinary (ik-STRAWR-dn-er-ee): beyond what is usual or ordinary

Memory Game

Can you match the image to what you read?

Index

Show What You Know

1. What does UFO stand for?
2. How long would it take to rocket to Proxima Centauri?
3. What happened in Roswell?
4. What happened to Alexander Hamilton's favorite cow?
5. What docs the Dogon tribe in Mali claim?

Further Reading

Aguilar, David A., *Alien Worlds: Your Guide to Extraterrestrial Life*, National Geographic Kids, 2013.

L'Engle, Madeleine, *A Wrinkle in Time*, Farrar, Straus and Giroux, 1962.

Patterson, J.W., *Kids Want to Know About: UFO's, Bigfoot, Mysterious Creatures, Mysterious Places, Mysterious People*, CreateSpace, 2016.

About the Author

Theo Baker is the author of several books for kids. He lives in Los Angeles with his wife and two daughters. He enjoys science, science fiction, and making weird noises into tape recorders.

Meet The Author!
www.meetREMauthors.com

www.rourkeeducationalmedia.com

PHOTO CREDITS: Cover, page 1: ©vchal; page3: ©m-gucci; page 4: ©Yuri_Arcuts; page 5: ©Ig0rZh; page 6: ©gmuttu; page 7: ©MicheleAlfieri; page 9: ©NASA; page 10: ©Lena_graphics; page 11: ©estt; page 12: ©jodijacobson; page 13: ©tomwachs; page 14: ©wiki; page 15: ©Fort Worth Star; page 16: ©MickeyCZ; page 17: ©Max2611; page 18: ©ianmcdonnell; page 19: ©Tashatuvango; page 20: ©bertos; page 21: ©Wiki; page 22: ©bertos; page 23: ©fergregory; page 25: ©homeworks255; page 26: ©RichVintage; page 27: ©Wiki; page 28: ©CladioVentrella; page 29: ©MatjazSlanic

Edited by: Keli Sipperley
Cover and interior design by: Kathy Walsh

Library of Congress PCN Data

Aliens and UFOs / Theo Baker
(Unexplained)
ISBN 978-1-64369-037-7 (hard cover)
ISBN 978-1-64369-101-5 (soft cover)
ISBN 978-1-64369-184-8 (e-Book)
Library of Congress Control Number: 2018955882

Rourke Educational Media
Printed in the United States of America,
North Mankato, Minnesota